'There isn't much time, thought Tom. 'But if I start straight away, I should be able to make a good costume.'

He knew what he wanted to be, and saw the first part of his disguise on Nonny's washing line. 'Nonny!' he called to his friend, 'can I borrow your shorts?'

'Yes - but what for?' Nonny called back.

'It's a secret!' replied Tom cheekily, as he rushed off.

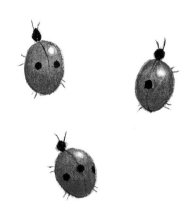

Tom Mouse peeped into Olivia's café. 'Hello!' he called. 'Anyone in?'

'Good morning,' said Olivia. 'What a fine day it is.'

Tom agreed. 'It's a fine day for borrowing two napkin rings and those sunglasses,' he said cheekily. 'Would that be alright?'

'Yes - but what for?' Olivia asked.

'It's a secret!' Tom replied as he rushed off.

On the way home, Tom bumped into a sleepy Ed Hedgehog.

'What will your disguise be?' Tom whispered in his friend's ear.

'Disguise?' said Ed. 'Let me think ... a creature that sleeps all the time.'

Tom laughed. 'You wouldn't need to dress up, Ed. That's you already!'

'But what would I be dressing up for?' Ed called after his friend.

'It's a secret!' replied Tom cheekily, as he rushed off.

All feeling rather curious, Ed, Nonny Frog and Olivia and Olly Owl decided to follow Tom to see what he was up to.

Can you find two napkin rings, a pair of sunglasses, some yellow flowers and the Ladybirds 1,2 and 3 in the big picture?

Can you spot a kite,
three worms and the
Ladybirds, 1 2 and 3 in
the big picture?

Soon, everyone had arrived at Tom and Ed's house, wondering what was going on. They all thought Tom's costume was brilliant. His favourite blue and white stripy shirt worked well for a pirate disguise - with all his friend's things added on top, of course.

'Oooh, arrgh, me hearties!' declared Tom between giggles.

'My shorts look great on your head!' said Nonny
Frog, laughing.

'I wondered what you wanted with those napkin
rings,' said Olivia. 'I don't think they will catch on!'

'Hooray!' said Tom, feeling pleased with himself.
'Now we need to find costumes for all of you. Let's
spend ten minutes gathering together all that we
can find and then see what we can make.'

Can you spot Nonny Frog, Ed Hedgehog, Olivia and Olly Owl, Kit Vole, and the Ladybirds 1, 2 and 3 in the big picture?

Don't the Country Companions look great
in their finished costumes, even the Ladybirds
have dressed up in stripes! Can you tell
what the other friends
are disguised as?

First published in Great Britain in 1999 by Madcap Books, André Deutsch Ltd, 76 Dean Street, London, W1V 5HA. www.vci.co.uk
Text and illustrations copyright © 1999 Madcap Books. Country Companions™ © Hallmark Cards UK